One very rainy day, Pan Pan comes looking for Fi Fi to see if she wants to play. She isn't on her lily pad, so Pan Pan goes to find her. He finally sees her hiding underneath a bush at the side of the pond.

THE LITTLE HELPERS
Pan Pan Helps Shelter From Acid Rain

Claire Cu~~lliford~~   Emma Allen

9112000052 0974

Pan Pan is a Panda. He's a cuddly-wuddly panda. Pan Pan is big, and black and white. Pan Pan is also a really affectionate panda. He loves giving his friends and family hugs.

Pan Pan lives in the mountains in China, in a bamboo forest. They are often covered in mist, which makes them look magical and mysterious.

Pan Pan has a lot of friends. His best friend is called Fi Fi and she's a frog. Fi Fi lives with her family on a lily pad in a pond in the mountains. Pan Pan is very big and Fi Fi is very small. Pan Pan likes sitting down a lot and Fi Fi likes jumping. But they both love playing together. Their favourite game is leapfrog, for obvious reasons! Fi Fi croaks with joy whenever they play it.

"Do you feel like a game of leapfrog?" Pan Pan asks Fi Fi.

Today though, Fi Fi doesn't look like she's jumping for joy. Her big frog mouth is turned down at the sides.

"I'm afraid I can't play anymore," she replies. "Mum and Dad say I have to stay under this bush because the rain has acid in it."

Pan Pan thinks he sees a tear running down Fi Fi's face. But it's hard to tell. It might just be a drop of rain.

"Why does it matter if the rain has acid in it?" asks Pan Pan, a little confused.

"Mum and dad say that the chemicals in the acid in the rain can hurt us," Fi Fi explains. "They can make it hard to fight off diseases and infections."

Pan Pan is really shocked when he hears this.

"How do we get rid of the acid in the rain?" he asks.

"We can't. My parents say that it's caused by things like smoke from factories and exhaust fumes from cars. To get rid of the acid in the rain, humans need to stop the smoke and the fumes being created. The best us animals can do for now is to shelter from the rain when it comes."

6

It rains a lot where Pan Pan and Fi Fi live. Now they won't be able to play leap frog together like before. They both sit quietly under the bush for a minute.

Pan Pan cares a lot about his friends. So, as the two animals sit together, he pulls a piece of bamboo from a bamboo bush and starts to chew on it. It helps him to think.

After a moment, Pan Pan suddenly throws his arms in the air.

"I've got it!" he says, grinning from ear to ear.
"I know how we can still play leapfrog, even when it's raining!"

And with that, Pan Pan slowly sways from side to side as he heaves himself upright. Standing his big panda body up takes a lot of energy. So he only does it when he really needs to! Then he very slowly strolls off.

Fi Fi wonders where Pan Pan has gone. After a short while, Pan Pan reappears, holding what looks like more bamboo.

"Where have you been?" asks Fi Fi.

"I went to get some of this," explains Pan Pan, holding up the long, slim bamboo sticks.

"You went to get food?" Fi Fi enquires, surprised that Pan Pan had thought this was the time to fill his belly.

"No, I got the bamboo to help you. We can use it to make a big shelter over the pond. It will protect you from the acid rain and we can play underneath it too!"

Fi Fi croaks with delight, and almost immediately the rest of her family appears.

"Is everything OK?" asks Fi Fi's dad.

Fi Fi explains Pan Pan's plan and the frogs all leap around with excitement.

"My dad wants to know if we can help you," asks Fi Fi.

"Yes please," replies Pan Pan. "My balance isn't that good so I could do with someone to make sure I don't fall over."

The family of frogs gather together to hold Pan Pan's legs firmly in place while he plants bamboo sticks around the edge of the pond. He then leans over and carefully places more bamboo sticks across the top. He ties reeds around them to keep all of the sticks in place.

"There," he says, "that should do it."

At just that moment, the rain starts again, so the frogs all hop underneath the new bamboo shelter. Not a drop of rain can reach them here, so they settle on their lily pads to wait for the rain to stop.

"Thank you so much," ribbits Fi Fi. "We can play leap frog again now!"

"I know," says Pan Pan, with a smile. He sinks his rather big behind back down to the floor again with a sigh.

"All this building is exhausting. Perhaps I'll just..."
And in a moment, Pan Pan can be heard snoring loudly
– ZZZZZ, ZZZZZ, ZZZZZ.

Fi Fi looks at him and, with a little shrug, starts happily leaping
back and forth over him. Because leapfrog is the game that
sleeping pandas and frogs play best too!

Questions for discussion

What causes acid rain?

Do you get acid rain where you live?

What other kinds of weather might cause
some problems for you and your friends?

University of Buckingham Press, 51 Gower Street, London, WC1E 6HJ
info@unibuckinghampress.com | www.unibuckinghampress.com

Text and Illustrations © Claire Culliford, 2022
Illustrations by Emma Allen, 2022

Print: 978-1-91505-464-7
Ebook: 978-1-91505-465-4

Set in Kabouter. Printed by St Austell Printing Company Ltd, Cornwall
Cover design and layout by Rachel Lawston, lawstondesign.com